THIS WALKER BOOK BELONGS TO:

_____

_____

_____

_____

For Mum and Dad ~ I.B.

First published 1996 by
Walker Books Ltd, 87 Vauxhall Walk
London SE11 5HJ

This edition published 1997

2 4 6 8 10 9 7 5 3

Text © 1996 Sam McBratney
Illustrations © 1996 Ivan Bates

The right of Sam McBratney to be
identified as the author of this work has been
asserted by him in accordance with the
Copyright, Designs and Patents Act 1988.

This book has been typeset in
Vernon Bold

Printed in Hong Kong

British Library Cataloguing
in Publication Data
A catalogue record for this book
is available from the British Library.

ISBN 0-7445-5405-5

THE DARK AT THE TOP OF THE STAIRS

Written by Sam McBratney
Illustrated by Ivan Bates

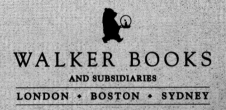

WALKER BOOKS

AND SUBSIDIARIES

LONDON • BOSTON • SYDNEY

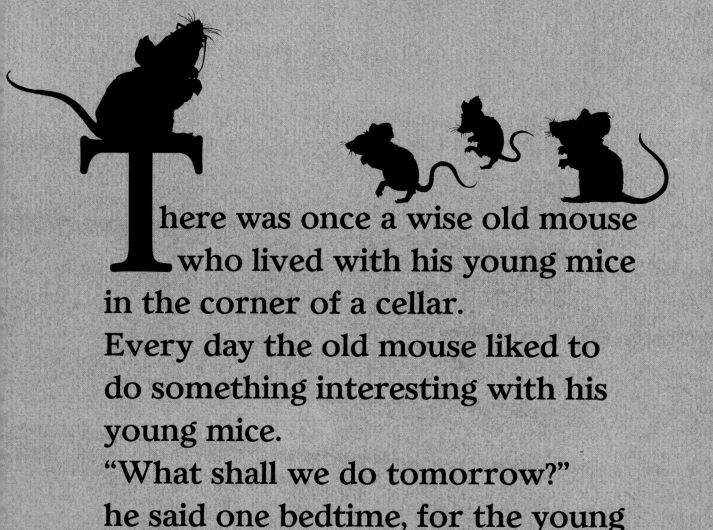

There was once a wise old mouse
who lived with his young mice
in the corner of a cellar.
Every day the old mouse liked to
do something interesting with his
young mice.
"What shall we do tomorrow?"
he said one bedtime, for the young
mice were getting ready to sleep
and he wanted them to look
forward to the morning.

"I would like to see the dark at the top of the stairs," said a young mouse whose name was Cob.

"Me too," said his sister Hazel, snuggling into the warm. "I want to see the dark at the top of the stairs."

"And so do I," said little Berry-Berry, the youngest of the three. "We've never been to the top of the big dark stairs where the monster lives." The old mouse thought for a while. It was true that he had not taken his young mice up the cellar stairs.

Then he said, "What about a walk
to the acorn tree in the garden?

Or a visit to your cousins in the
cornfield? We could even have
a swing on the seed-heads
of the long grass."

"No," said Cob. "We want to see the dark at the top of the stairs."

"Or we'll climb up there on our own," said Hazel.

"And see the monster by ourselves!" laughed little Berry-Berry.

The old mouse nodded as he made his young mice comfortable in their bed.

"Very well then, we will go there in the morning," he said.

He spoke as if he knew that sooner or later all young mice will try to see the dark at the top of the stairs.

In the morning, as early sunshine lit up the cobwebs in the corners of the cellar windows, they set out on their journey.

"Let's not talk about the monster," whispered Cob on the third step up. "I won't mention it if you don't mention it," whispered Hazel. "I won't talk about the monster either," laughed little Berry-Berry, who hadn't learned how to whisper yet.

After seven steps they stopped once more. There was excitement in their eyes, and the young mice hardly dared to look up, for they were closer now than they had ever been to the dark at the top of the stairs. "I wonder if it's really really real?" whispered Cob.

"You said you wouldn't talk about it," whispered Hazel.

"I hope the monster knows we're coming!" cried little Berry-Berry.

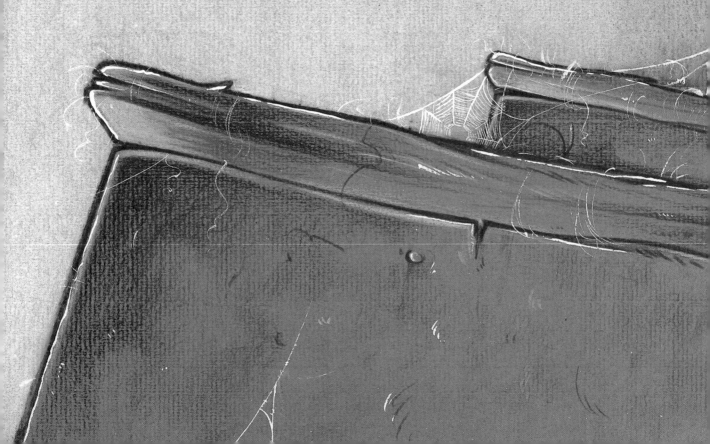

On the tenth step up, only two from the top, they paused once more. Hazel turned to the old mouse and whispered, "What is the monster like? Is it the most terrible thing anyone has ever seen?"

"We haven't far to go now," the old mouse said, and climbed the last two steps. After him came Hazel and Cob and finally little Berry-Berry, who said, "I don't see any monster at the top of the stairs."

Then something
happened.
The young mice
crept into a crack
of light . . .

They saw a monster shadow move towards them as smoothly as a cloud, and something breathed out softly one strange word:

M I A O W

The young mice did
not wait to say goodbye.
With wildly beating
hearts they went . . .

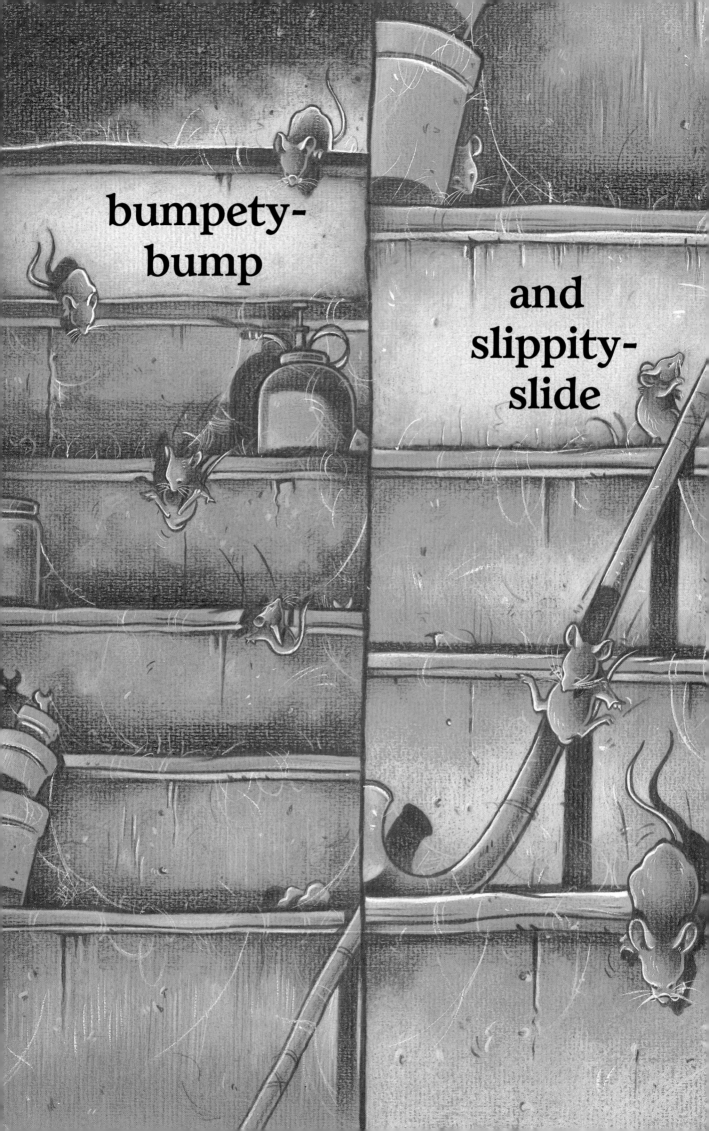

bumpety-
bump

and
slippity-
slide

and tumble-thump

all the way to the bottom of the stairs, where they landed in a wriggle and a heap before making a dash for warm, safe, wonderful home.

At the end of the day the old mouse came to ask his young mice what they would like to do tomorrow.

"I would like to go to the acorn tree," said Cob.

"I would like to visit our cousins in the cornfield," said Hazel.

"I would like to swing backwards and forwards on the long grass!" said little Berry-Berry.

But none of them mentioned the dark at the top of the stairs.

MORE WALKER PAPERBACKS
For You to Enjoy

THE PARK IN THE DARK
by Martin Waddell/Barbara Firth

Winner of the Kurt Maschler Award

A delightful bedtime story about the spooky night-time adventures
of three soft toys – a monkey, an elephant and a little dog.

"Remember *Can't You Sleep, Little Bear?* This book is even better."
Books for Keeps

0-7445-1740-0 £4.99

DAISY DARE
by Anita Jeram

Daisy Dare is a very brave mouse. She's not scared of anything, she says.
But will she dare take the bell off the cat's collar? Find out in this
delightful tale – by the illustrator of *Guess How Much I Love You* –
in The Giggle Club – a series of inexpensive story books for early readers.

0-7445-4783-0 £1.99

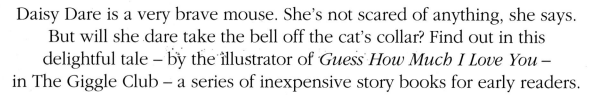

OWL BABIES
by Martin Waddell/Patrick Benson

On a tree in the dark woods, three baby owls, Sarah and Percy and Bill,
wait for their Owl Mother to come home.

"Touchingly beautiful... Drawn with exquisite delicacy... The perfect picture book."
The Guardian

0-7445-3167-5 £4.50